My Beliefs

By

Kirsty Holmes

Crabtree Publishing Company

www.crabtreebooks.com

1-800-387-7650

Published in Canada
Crabtree Publishing
616 Welland Avenue
St. Catharines, ON
L2M 5V6

Published in the United States
Crabtree Publishing
PMB 59051
350 Fifth Ave, 59th Floor
New York, NY 10118

Published by Crabtree Publishing Company in 2018

First Published by Book Life in 2018
Copyright © 2018 Book Life

Author: Kirsty Holmes

Editors: Holly Duhig, Janine Deschenes

Design: Daniel Scase

Proofreader: Petrice Custance

**Production coordinator and
 prepress technician (interior):** Margaret Amy Salter

Prepress technician (covers): Ken Wright

Print coordinator: Margaret Amy Salter

Printed in the USA/012018/BG20171102

Photographs
Abbreviations: l-left, r-right, b-bottom,
t-top, c-centre, m-middle.

Front cover - KK Tan. 2 – espies. 4 – Yuganov Konstantin.
5 – KonstantinChristian. 6 – ESB Professional. 7 – alphaspirit.
8 – India Picture. 9 – Sergieiev. 10 – natushm. 11 – Zurijeta. 12 – Anneka.
13 – Food Photography for Biz. 14 – Howard Sandler. 15 – FamVeld.
16 – wavebreakmedia. 17 – Mrs_ya. 18 – Eakwiphan Smitabhindhu.
19 – Andrew Roland. 20 – ZouZou. 21 – Monkey Business Images.
22 – Rawpixel.com. 23 – Inara Prusakova
Images are courtesy of Shutterstock.com. With thanks to Getty Images,
Thinkstock Photo and iStockphoto.

Library and Archives Canada Cataloguing in Publication

Holmes, Kirsty Louise, author
        My beliefs / Kirsty Holmes.

(Our values)
Includes index.
Issued in print and electronic formats.
ISBN 978-0-7787-4727-7 (hardcover).--
ISBN 978-0-7787-4742-0 (softcover).--
ISBN 978-1-4271-2080-9 (HTML)

        1. Respect for persons--Juvenile literature. 2. Respect--Juvenile
literature. 3. Freedom of religion--Juvenile literature. 4. Values--Juvenile
literature. 5. Toleration--Juvenile literature. I. Title.

BJ1533.R4H65 2018   j179'.9   C2017-906915-2
                                            C2017-906916-0

Library of Congress Cataloging-in-Publication Data

CIP available at the Library of Congress

Contents

Words that look like **this** can be found in the glossary on page 24.

What is a Belief?

A belief is something that is accepted, or trusted, to be true.

If you have a belief in something, you think it is real or true, even if you can't see, hear, or touch it.

Many people share the same beliefs as their family or people in their community.

Different Beliefs

People follow many different religions. Each one has their own beliefs. Many religions believe that there is a god or gods.

Jewish

Sikh

Christian

Muslim

Buddhist

Hindu

Some people do not follow a religion at all. They are atheist.

Atheists do not believe in any god. But they can still have other beliefs.

Religious beliefs are often written in books. Followers of a religion read the books to learn about their beliefs.

Elias follows the religion of Islam. He reads a book called the Qur'ān.

Christian beliefs are written in a book called the Bible.

Sam's dad reads her stories from the Bible.

9

Showing Beliefs

Many people wear special clothes or jewelry to show their beliefs.

Ezra is Jewish. He wears a special cap, called a kippah, when he prays or studies his religion.

Some people use **symbols** as a way of showing their beliefs.

Sarah's crucifix necklace is a symbol of her Christian beliefs. A crucifix is a cross with Jesus Christ on it.

Many people choose to cover their hair or head. This shows **respect** for their religion.

Mohan's family are Sikh. Sikh boys and men cover their hair with a cloth called a turban.

Mo's mother wears a hijab to cover her head. She is Muslim.

Celebrating Beliefs

Most religions have special days to celebrate their beliefs. Diwali is a Hindu celebration. It lasts for five days. It is a **festival** of lights.

Hanukkah is a Jewish celebration. A new candle is lit on each of the eight days of the festival. Can you count them?

The ninth candle is used for lighting the others.

Worship and Belief

Beliefs are very important to people. People who believe in a god or gods might worship them.

Worship means to show respect to your god.

Some people worship by praying. This means they think quietly about the god they believe in.

Muslims often pray on a special rug.

Places of Worship

Many religions have a special building where people gather together to worship and pray.

At Hindu temples, everyone takes off their shoes!

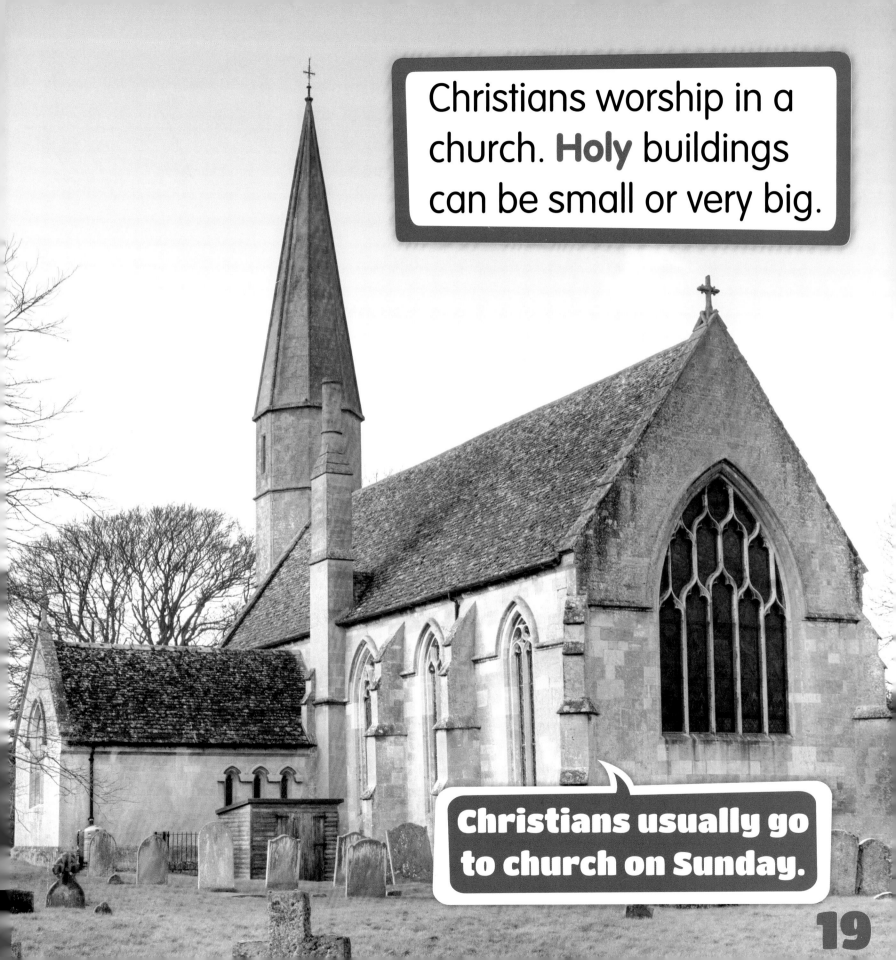

Christians worship in a church. **Holy** buildings can be small or very big.

Christians usually go to church on Sunday.

Places of worship can be important to a community. People often get married in them.

Everyone has different beliefs. Even people with the same religion can believe different things.

Respecting Beliefs

We should always respect other people's beliefs.

Do your friends and their families have different beliefs than you?

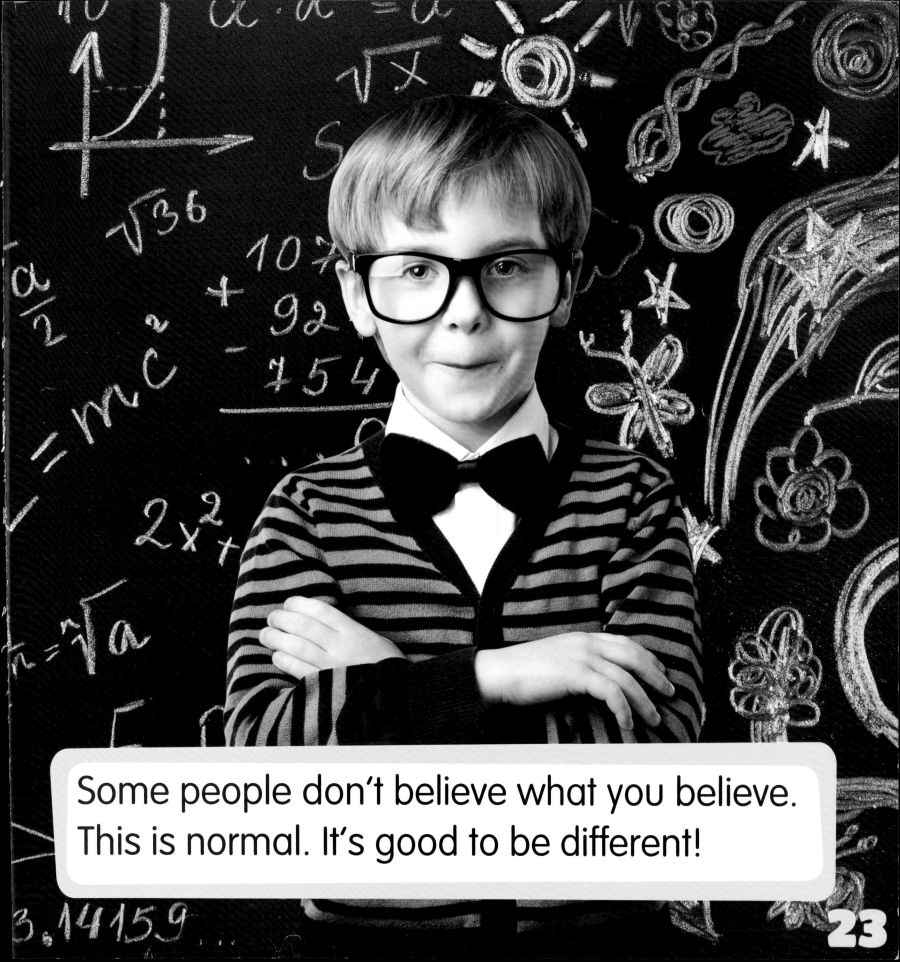

Some people don't believe what you believe. This is normal. It's good to be different!

Glossary

community	A group of people who live, work, and play in the same area
festival	A time when people come together to celebrate special events
holy	Related to a god or special to a religion
religion	The belief in and worship of a god or gods
respect	A feeling that someone or something is good and important
symbols	A thing that represents something else

Index